The Traditional Tale

JACK
AND THE
BEANSTALK

As Told By

TIM PAULSON

Illustrated By Mark Corcoran

Here is Jack's version of this famous story.
Turn the book over and read the story from the Giant's point of view

A Citadel Press Book
Published by Carol Publishing Group

First Carol Publishing Group Edition 1992

A Citadel Press Book
Published by Carol Publishing Group
Citadel Press is a registered trademark of Carol Communications, Inc.

Editorial Offices : 600 Madison Avenue, New York, NY 10022
Sales & Distribution Offices: 120 Enterprise Avenue, Secaucus, NJ 07094
In Canada: Canadian Manda Group, P.O. Box 920, Station U, Toronto,
Ontario, M8Z 5P9, Canada

Queries regarding rights and permissions should be addressed to Carol
Publishing Group, 600 Madison Avenue, New York, NY 10022

Manufactured in the United States of America
ISBN 0-8065-1313-6

Carol Publishing Group books are available at special discounts
for bulk purchases, for sales promotions, fund raising, or
educational purposes. Special editions can also be created to
specifications. For details contact: Special Sales Department,
Carol Publishing Group, 120 Enterprise Ave., Secaucus, NJ 07094

10 9 8 7 6 5 4 3 2 1

Library of Congress Cataloging-in-Publication Data

Paulsen, Tim.
    Jack and the beanstalk and the beanstalk incident/ Tim Paulsen;
illustrated by Mark Corcoran.
        p.   cm.
     Summary: After reading the classic tale of Jack and the Beanstalk,
the reader is invited to turn the book upside down and read an updated
version told from the giant's vantage point.
            1. Toy and movable books--Specimens.   [1. Fairy tales.
    2. Folklore--England.   3. Giants--Folklore.   4. Toy and movable
books.] I. Corcoran, Mark, ill.   II. Title.   III. Title: Beanstalk incident.

PZ8.P282Jac   1990
[398.2]--dc20   90-41897
                                                           CIP
                                                            AC

JACK
AND THE
BEANSTALK

Once upon a time, in a tumbledown cottage, there lived a poor widow and her son Jack. One day, when there was nothing left to eat, Jack's mother decided they had to sell their only possession, a milk cow named Whitey.

"Be sure to get a good price for the cow," Jack's mother told him, "for she is all we have left."

So Jack took Whitey and set out for town. He had never been to market alone before, and he was very excited.

On the way to market Jack met a strange-looking man. "What a handsome cow," the man said. "I'll trade you these magic beans for it." And the man held out five beans for Jack to look at.

"Magic beans," cried Jack. "It's a trade!" And he ran home proudly. But when he told his mother what had happened, she was not happy.

"Magic beans!" she shouted. "How could you, Jack? You traded the last thing we own in the world for a handful of beans!" She was so angry, she threw the beans right out the window.

That night Jack went to bed feeling very hungry and miserable.

When he awoke the next morning, Jack saw an amazing sight outside his bedroom window.

"A giant beanstalk!" he yelled. "As high as the sky!"

In no time, Jack was climbing up the beanstalk to see what was there.

Jack climbed and climbed, until he climbed right up through the clouds. There, to his amazement, he saw a great castle floating on a cloud.

Jack stepped very carefully off the beanstalk. When he did not fall through the clouds, he began to walk, then run, straight for the castle.

When Jack finally reached the castle door, he found it was so big he could not reach the handle. So he shouted as loud as he could, "Hello! Is anybody home?"

Suddenly the door opened, and there stood a giantess. Jack had never seen a giant before, and he wasn't sure he wanted to now. But before he could blink, she had scooped him up and carried him into her kitchen.

"I wondered what that squeaking was," the giantess said. "Hello, little thing." Her voice was so loud, it hurt Jack's ears. "You've come just in time," she continued. "We'd love to have you for dinner."

Then Jack heard a booming voice from deep in the castle:

"FE FIE FO FUM!
I SMELL THE BLOOD OF AN ENGLISHMAN.
BE HE ALIVE, OR BE HE DEAD,
I'LL GRIND HIS BONES TO MAKE MY
    BREAD!"

Jack shivered. He wasn't about to be anyone's dinner. Bravely he bit the giantess's thumb as hard as he could.

"Ouch!" she yelped. Jack leaped onto the kitchen table and scrambled into an enormous bowl of fruit.

Jack hid behind the biggest pears he had ever seen. Just then the giant came thundering into the kitchen. "What's for dinner, my wife?" he boomed.

"Sheep stew, dear," the giantess replied. "I found a tiny little boy this afternoon. I hoped to have him for dinner, but he ran away." Trembling, Jack crouched down lower behind the pears.

The giantess served up two monstrous bowls filled with hunks of meat as big as Jack's head and carrots the size of logs. The giants gnashed their teeth and smacked their lips, and ate and ate. After they had finished, the giant said, "Fetch my goose that lays the golden eggs." His wife brought to the table a goose that was almost as big as Jack himself.

"Lay," the giant commanded. And the goose laid a golden egg.

"Lay!" he said again. And the goose laid another perfect golden egg.

After the third time, the giants' heads began to nod, and soon they fell asleep right at the table.

The giants were snoring now. The goose was asleep, too. Jack stared at it and thought about the golden eggs. With a goose like that, he thought, he and his mother would no longer have any money problems. Jack made up his mind to steal the goose.

Carefully, he crept from the bowl and tiptoed across the table. As quickly and as quietly as he could, he grabbed the goose under his arm and turned to run. As soon as he did, the goose let out a startled HONK! The giants woke up at once!

Holding tight to the goose, Jack made a daring leap off the table. Then he raced across the kitchen and out the castle door with the giant close behind.

"Stop! Come back with my goose that lays the golden eggs!" the giant yelled as he ran after Jack.

But Jack didn't even stop for breath. He tore out across the clouds, jumped onto the beanstalk, and began climbing down through the clouds. The giant followed him. His big body caused the beanstalk to sway from side to side.

At last, Jack reached the bottom. Grabbing an axe, he chopped at the beanstalk as hard as he could.

Finally, with a great groan, the beanstalk came
crashing to the ground.

There was an enormous BOOM! When the dust
settled, Jack saw the giant lying at the bottom of a
giant hole.

As soon as Jack told his mother about his adventure, they went off to the market. They bought bread and cheese and jam, a new cow and a few chickens, and some beans (not magic ones) to start a garden with. And they paid for everything with a shiny golden egg.

When they got home, the giant was gone, and they never saw him again. And that was fine with them—especially Jack, who never forgot how it felt to almost be a giant's dinner.

Now, that's the way Jack tells the story. But those who live in the castle tell the tale a little differently. Turn this book over if you want to hear their side of the story.

The first thing we saw the next morning was another giant beanstalk! I never knew Alvin could be so nimble, for we were back in the clouds quicker than you could say Edwina's cherry frappé pudding.

Edwina was waiting at the top, already planning breakfast *and* lunch. "After the bacon and maple syrup rolls, we'll have the sausage pie and fried chicken with biscuits and apricot marmalade and fresh lemonade. And, Lucille, I didn't forget the seed cakes!"

Then Edwina stopped. "But first," she said, "we're going to pull up this beanstalk. No guests today—especially ones named Jack!"

So we pulled up the beanstalk, and we've never seen Jack since. And that's fine with us. We just hope he never meets a strange-looking man with magic beans to trade.

We decided to take a golden egg to market to trade for food. On the way, though, we met a strange-looking man.

"What a beautiful golden egg," he admired. "I'll trade you these five magic beans for it."

"Magic . . . bah!" I snorted to myself. But Alvin is very trusting and he made the deal. Unfortunately, he forgot to find out what the beans did. He tried to eat them, but they were hard and hurt his teeth. "Phoot!" He spit them out onto the ground. Then, hungry and miserable, we fell asleep.

"Go back, Alvin!" I shouted. "Go back!" But before Alvin could turn around, Jack chopped right through that thick beanstalk, and it fell over with a thundering crash.

Of course, Alvin also fell—BOOM!—and made a giant hole in the ground.

Jack and his mother went right off to market, leaving me nothing but cold water and hard kernels of corn for dinner. I was longing for one of Edwina's seed cakes when I saw Alvin's head pop up out of the giant hole in the ground. "Oh, Alvin," I cried, "you have an awful lump on your head!"

"Never mind," he said glumly. "I'm too hungry to hurt."

Jack jumped into a hole in the clouds and began climbing down a giant beanstalk. When I looked down I nearly fainted. It was miles to the ground! Then I looked up to see Alvin diving through the hole after us. Alvin isn't small and he made the beanstalk shake and sway so much I just knew we were all going to fall!

At last, Jack and I made it to the ground. Then, to my horror, he picked up an axe and started chopping down the beanstalk.

Thinking that they had finally made their guest happy, the two giants fell asleep, exhausted. Soon, I was asleep too. Jack had worn us all out.

Suddenly I woke up. Jack had me by the neck and was dragging me across the table. The ungrateful boy was stealing me!

"Help! Help!" I honked, and the giants woke up.

"Stop!" yelled Alvin, quite forgetting to whisper. "Come back! Give me back our goose that lays the golden eggs!" But Jack just kept on running.

"Ouch!" said Alvin, remembering to whisper just in time.

The giants were desperate. They had never failed so miserably at entertaining a guest.

"The goose!" cried Alvin. "He's sure to love the goose!" And so I nervously sat on the table and laid three perfect golden eggs. Jack quieted down immediately at the sight of the eggs. He even began to smile.

"Edwina," whispered Alvin, dodging a radish,
"maybe our guest is trying to tell us he wants to play a
game. How about some Chinese checkers?"

"Of course," Edwina exclaimed softly. "Why didn't
I think of that." But as soon as she set up the board on
the table, Jack sent marbles rolling every which way
onto the floor. Poor Alvin slipped on one and crashed
to the ground, smashing a chair.

Edwina's sheep stew had always been a hit with guests, but Jack didn't seem to like it at all. When Edwina served him a bowl, he jumped up and down on the spoon. Then he laughed as the meat and carrots went flying everywhere, nearly hitting me! "Oh dear," Edwina muttered nervously to Alvin. "Perhaps it's too salty."

When she put down a plate of seed cakes and radishes, the little brat began throwing the radishes at the giants. Alvin and Edwina didn't know what to think!

"Well, my dear," Edwina said, nodding toward the bowl of fruit, "we have a guest for dinner." Then she tried to introduce Alvin to the boy. "Alvin," she began, "this is . . . ahhh . . . I don't believe I heard your name, little boy."

"Jack!" the boy shrieked. "And I do wish you would speak more softly. Your big, loud voices are hurting my ears."

So for the rest of the evening the two giants whispered for the boy's comfort.

Edwina hurried to set another place at the table, thinking that her guest was starving. Just then Alvin ambled in singing one of his favorite songs:

FE FIE FOE FUM!
WE START EACH DAY WITH HOT CROSS
    BUNS.
EDWINA LOVES TO KEEP US FED,
WITH SEED CAKES, SHEPHERD'S PIE, AND
    BREAD.

Alvin's eyes widened when he spotted the tiny boy biting the pear, but he tried not to stare. Like Edwina, Alvin is very polite.

make faces, but Edwina thought perhaps he was just shy. So she tried to put him at ease.

"You've come just in time," she smiled. "We'd love to have you for dinner." Now, most people would have answered, "Thank you very much." But this boy leaned over and bit Edwina's thumb! Then he jumped onto the table and dived into the bowl of fruit.

After a moment he began to take bites out of one of the pears, pretending that no one could see what he was doing. Whoever this boy was, he certainly had no manners.

The day Jack came, Edwina was making a pot of delicious sheep stew for dinner. Suddenly she heard a squeaking noise at the kitchen door. To her surprise, she found a very tiny boy standing outside. She couldn't hear what he was squeaking about, so she scooped him up in her hand and brought him close to her ear.

"Hello, little thing," she said politely. But the boy only scowled. I was always taught that it was rude to

The truth is, Alvin and Edwina are friendly folks
who like nothing better than to have guests over for
dinner and a game of Chinese checkers. But one day
they had an uninvited guest who almost changed their
minds about entertaining. And that guest was Jack.

You have probably heard the story of Jack
who climbed a magic beanstalk up to the clouds and
met two evil giants. But I'll bet you've never heard the
giants' side of this tale. I know it well, because I'm
Lucille, their goose that lays the golden eggs. And I
have lived with the giants (whose names are Alvin
and Edwina) since way before once upon a time.

Now, some giants are ferocious and eat small
children, but not Alvin and Edwina. True, they love
to cook and eat, but only things like tea cakes. Never
little children!

THE
BEANSTALK
INCIDENT

First Carol Publishing Group Edition 1992

A Citadel Press Book
Published by Carol Publishing Group
Citadel Press is a registered trademark of Carol Communications, Inc.

Editorial Offices : 600 Madison Avenue, New York, NY 10022
Sales & Distribution Offices: 120 Enterprise Avenue, Secaucus, NJ 07094
In Canada: Canadian Manda Group, P.O. Box 920, Station U, Toronto,
Ontario, M8Z 5P9, Canada

Queries regarding rights and permissions should be addressed to Carol
Publishing Group, 600 Madison Avenue, New York, NY 10022

Manufactured in the United States of America
ISBN 0-8065-1313-6

Carol Publishing Group books are available at special discounts
for bulk purchases, for sales promotions, fund raising, or
educational purposes. Special editions can also be created to
specifications. For details contact: Special Sales Department,
Carol Publishing Group, 120 Enterprise Ave., Secaucus, NJ 07094

10 9 8 7 6 5 4 3 2 1

Library of Congress Cataloging-in-Publication Data

Paulsen, Tim.
    Jack and the beanstalk and the beanstalk incident/ Tim Paulsen;
illustrated by Mark Corcoran.
        p.   cm.
        Summary: After reading the classic tale of Jack and the Beanstalk,
the reader is invited to turn the book upside down and read an updated
version told from the giant's vantage point.
            1. Toy and movable books--Specimen   [1. Fairy tales.
2. Folklore--England. 3. Giants--Folklore. 4. Toy and movable
books.] I. Corcoran, Mark, ill. II. Title. III. Title: Beanstalk incident.

PZ8.P282Jac   1990
[398.2]---dc20   90-41897
                                                    CIP
                                                    AC

UPSIDE DOWN TALES

The Giant's Story

THE BEANSTALK INCIDENT

TIM PAULSON

Illustrated By Mark Corcoran

Here is the Giant's version of this famous story

Turn the book over and read the story from Jack's point of view

A Citadel Press Book
Published by Carol Publishing Group